the alphabet tree

Leo Lionni

Dragonfly Books ——⚹— **New York**

"This is the Alphabet Tree," said the ant.
"Why is it called the Alphabet Tree?" asked
his friend.

"Because not so long ago this tree was full of letters. They lived a happy life, hopping from leaf to leaf on the highest twigs.

Each letter had its favorite leaf, where it would sit in the sun and rock in the gentle breeze of spring.

One day the breeze became a strong gust and the gust became a gale.

The letters clung to the leaves with all their might—but some were blown away, and the others were very frightened.

When the storm had passed they huddled together in fear, deep in the foliage of the lower branches.

A funny bug, red and black with
bright yellow wings, saw them there,
hiding in the shade.
'We are hiding from the wind,'
the letters explained. 'But who are you?'
'I am the word-bug,' the bug answered.
'I can teach you to make words.
If you get together in threes and fours,
and even more,
no wind will be strong enough
to blow you away.'

Patiently he taught the letters to join together and make words.

men

Some made short and easy words like *dog* and *cat*, others learned to make more difficult ones: *twig*, *leaf*, and even *earth*.

twig

wind

green

Happily they climbed back onto the highest leaves, and when the wind came they held on without fear. The word-bug had been right.

peace

on good

tree

men and

red will

earth

w

Then, one summer morning, a strange caterpillar appeared amid the foliage. He was purple, woolly, and very large. 'Such confusion!' said the caterpillar when he saw the words scattered around the leaves. 'Why don't you get together and make sentences—and *mean* something?'

The letters had never thought of this. Now they could really write—*say* things. They said things about the wind, the leaves, the bug. 'Good!' said the caterpillar approvingly. 'But not good enough.'

the wind is bad

leaves are green

the bug is small

the

'Why?' asked the letters, surprised.
'Because you must say something *important*,'
said the caterpillar.

peace on earth and

The letters tried to think of something important, *really* important. Finally they knew what to say. What could be more important than peace? PEACE ON EARTH AND GOODWILL TOWARD ALL MEN, they spelled excitedly.

will toward all men

'Great!' said the caterpillar. 'Now climb onto my back.' One by one the letters climbed onto the woolly back. 'But where are you taking us?' they asked anxiously, as the caterpillar began climbing down the tree.

'To the President,' said the caterpillar."

peace

About the Author

Leo Lionni, an internationally known designer, illustrator, and graphic artist, was born in Holland and studied in Italy until he came to the United States in 1939. He was the recipient of the 1984 American Institute of Graphic Arts Gold Medal and was honored posthumously in 2007 with the Society of Illustrators Lifetime Achievement Award. His picture books are distinguished by their enduring moral themes, graphic simplicity, and brilliant use of collage, and include four Caldecott Honor Books: *Inch by Inch*, *Frederick*, *Swimmy*, and *Alexander and the Wind-Up Mouse*. Hailed as "a master of the simple fable" by the *Chicago Tribune*, he died in 1999 at the age of 89.

All rights reserved. Published in the United States by Dragonfly Books,
an imprint of Random House Children's Books,
a division of Random House, Inc., New York. Originally published in hardcover
in the United States by Pantheon Books, a division of Random House, Inc., New York, in 1968.

Dragonfly Books with the colophon is a registered trademark of Random House, Inc.

Visit us on the Web! www.randomhouse.com/kids
Educators and librarians, for a variety of teaching tools, visit us at www.randomhouse.com/teachers

The Library of Congress has cataloged the hardcover edition of this work as follows:

Lionni, Leo. The alphabet tree / Leo Lionni. p. cm.
Summary: After a storm blows some of them away, the letters on the alphabet tree learn from a strange bug to be stronger by forming words.
Then a caterpillar comes along and tells them that words are not enough; they must say something important.
ISBN 978-0-394-81016-4 (trade) — ISBN 978-0-394-91016-1 (lib. bdg.) — ISBN 978-0-679-80835-0 (pbk.)
[1. Alphabet—Fiction. 2. Writing—Fiction. 3. Insects—Fiction. 4. Caterpillars—Fiction.] I. Title.   PZ7.L6634A1 2004   [E]—dc22   2003016215

MANUFACTURED IN CHINA
33 32 31 30 29 28 27 26

Random House Children's Books supports the First Amendment and celebrates the right to read.

Peta
ar Goll

Peta
gets Lost

Jane Griffiths-Jones

Gomer

Bob dydd mae Peta Pengwin yn mynd
allan i chwarae ar yr iâ gwyn llachar.

Every day Peta Pengwin goes off to play on the bright white ice.

A bob dydd mae Mam yn dweud:

'Cofia nawr, 'nghyw bach i, cadw draw oddi wrth y creaduriaid

mawr llwglyd a'r llethrau llithrig serth a'r môr mawr glas!'

And every day Mum says:
'Remember this, my little chick. Try and stay away from the big hungry
creatures and the steep slippy slopes and the deep blue sea!'

'Wrth gwrs!' meddai Peta gan wenu.

'I will!' Peta says smiling.

Ond un bore oer a rhewllyd
anghofiodd Peta am eiriau Mam a
neidiodd ar ben morlo mawr llwglyd.

But one cold and frosty morning Peta forgot what Mum
had said and he hopped on to a big hungry sea lion.

Ac aeth i chwarae ar lethr llithrig serth...

And he slid down a steep slippy slope...

A syrthiodd i mewn i'r môr mawr glas.

And he fell into the deep blue sea.

Roedd siarcod syn yn nofio rownd a rownd.

Stary scary sharks swam round and round.

Ac roedd adar mawr llwglyd yn

plymio ac yn crawcian...

And big hungry birds swooped down and squawked...

'O diar,' meddai Peta, 'dwi eisiau mynd adre.'

'Oh dear,' cried Peta, 'I want to go home.'

'Paid â phoeni, bengwin bach,' chwythodd morfil.

'Dere gyda fi ac fe allwn ni neidio a chwythu

bob cam adre gyda'n gilydd.'

'There, there, little penguin. Don't be scared,' spouted a whale.
'Come with me and we will leap and spout together all the way home.'

'Paid â chrio,' chwarddodd octopws.
'Dere gyda fi ac fe allwn ni badlo a phlymio
bob cam adre gyda'n gilydd.'

'Don't cry, little penguin,' gurgled an octopus. 'Just follow me
and we will paddle and gurgle together all the way home.'

'Paid â bod yn drist, bengwin bach,' cleciodd dolffin.

'Dere gyda fi ac fe allwn ni sblasio a chlecio

bob cam adre gyda'n gilydd.'

'Don't be sad, little penguin,' clicked a dolphin.
'We will splash and click together all the way home.'

Felly dyma nhw'n padlo ac yn plymio...

And so they paddled and gurgled...

Ac yn sblasio ac yn clecio...

And they splashed and they clicked...

28

Ac yn neidio ac yn chwythu bob cam adre...

And they leapt and they spouted all the way home...

29

'Ble wyt ti wedi bod, 'nghyw bach i?'
holodd Mam yn llawn gofid.

'Where have you been, my little chick?'
asked Mum looking worried.

'Wel, fe fues i'n nofio yn y môr mawr glas gyda
llawer o greaduriaid mawr llwglyd,' atebodd Peta.
'Ond dwi wedi gwneud sawl ffrind newydd,'
meddai gan wenu.

'I slid into the deep blue sea and I had to swim
with lots of scary things,' spouted Peta.
'But I have made lots of new friends,' he said smiling.